Wishing on a Rainbow

D1520220

Thomas Yorke

ISBN: 1518857604

ISBN 13: 9781518857607

Library of Congress Control Number:
2015918362

CreateSpace Independent Publishing

North Charleston, South Carolina USA

DEDICATION

For Alison, Sophie, and a new arrival
in May. You will always be my babies.

CONTENTS

ACKNOWLEDGMENTS

I want to thank my editor Deanna Yorke. She was able to maintain her sanity though out all my many rewrites and revisions, even though each required re-editing for her. Deanna helped keep me focused and eliminated unimportant detail and distractions.

I want to thank my family: George, Melissa, Alison, Tom, Deanna, Sophie, and a baby due in May 2016, and my wife Nancy who helped me to understand that you can do anything if you try hard enough. The impossible sometimes just takes a little longer.
.

PREFACE

The Oklahoma Land Rush gave every man the opportunity to stake his claim to a piece of the American Dream. Sooners and Boomers, winners and losers, the hearty and the hardscrabble, all raced westward in the hope of finding their own little piece of paradise. For Mark and Junior, two young men who were just coming of age at the dawn of this new century, life presented them with a different set of circumstances. How can you decide when your friend needs your help, your family is counting on you, and your country may be going to war? And what are all of these historical figures doing here in Enid, Oklahoma?

Legend states that at the end of the rainbow lies a pot of gold. Most people say this isn't true, but then most people have never tried wishing on a rainbow. Hopes and dreams are riches far more valuable than any mere pot of gold. And, you might not have to go wishing on a rainbow to find them. Everything you ever wanted might have been right here all along. All you have to do is open your eyes.

This story takes place well over a hundred years ago. There are many things that were quite different back then. However, there are also many things that haven't changed at all: friends and family, love and loyalty, and even bias and prejudice. Our ability to understand, adapt, live and learn from them will always be a part of our life.

1. The Cherokee Outlet

Walter McClain had been a trail boss on the Chisholm Trail for most of his life. The Chisholm Trail was one of the many well-traveled paths used by cattle drives to move their herds from Texas north to the railroads in Kansas. Walter had started as a horse wrangler while he was still in his teens. He was in charge of what they called the remuda, or spare horses. Cowboys usually needed at least three horses each for a successful cattle drive, so the availability of fresh horses was critical. Walter worked his way up to cowboy and then to trail boss, becoming one of the youngest ever in the history of the western cattle trails.

Walter was a tall and powerful man. While his size and strength made for an intimidating first impression, he always handled himself with dignity and treated everyone with respect. He was an honest and religous man. As a trail boss, he would not abide with any hell raising or alcohol use by his men. Walter said that whatever they did after the drive was between them, their God, and the devil. His integrity and strength of character put him in high demand by cattle owners looking to move their herds. Walter had a loyal crew of cowboys whom he employed whenever possible. He needed to know he could trust his men, and they needed to know what was expected of them.

Lamont "Doc" Johnson had driven the chuck wagon on Walter McClain's cattle drives for almost twenty years. If the trail boss was the most important man on a cattle drive, the chuck wagon master was easily second. He was in charge of the food, extra horse tack, bedrolls, and blankets. He even had a few medical responsibilities. That's how he got the name "Doc." If you were brave, you could try calling him "Cookie" or "Lamont," but if you did, you could expect to find a snake in your saddlebags. Doc had served in the Union army during the war, and it was said he was part of the security detail that searched for Abraham Lincoln's assassin after he was shot and killed in 1865. Doc never spoke much about his army days, but loved to talk about almost anything else.

The McClain-Johnson relationship had one more important connection. In 1881, Walter McClain married Doc's kid sister, Julie Johnson. Soon after they added two fine sons to their family. Walter made a good living working on cattle drives, but this life meant he had to spend much of his time away from home. Julie and the boys lived at her parents' old farmhouse in Abilene with her two older sisters. Walter tried to see his family whenever he could, but he knew the boys were growing up and needed a male role model. He decided it was time to leave the cattle drive life and find a place to settle down. He had always dreamed of starting his own cattle ranch and maybe this was his chance.

The Cherokee Outlet was six million acres of prime grazing land, located east of the Chisholm Trail and south of Kansas in the Oklahoma Territory. This area had been designated as a pathway for the Cherokee Indian nation, giving them access to the buffalo hunting grounds in the West from their US government-designated reservations in the East. This area had also been used for grazing cattle to fatten them before moving on to the railroads in Kansas. From there, they were shipped to the slaughterhouses of Kansas City, St. Louis, and Chicago. Many people thought this land was far too valuable to be left only to the Indians and cattle drives, and they clamored it was needed for homesteading. When the federal government obliged and began to make plans to open up the area to settlers, Walter decided this presented his best opportunity to make a home and a life for his family.

Walter knew this land very well and had been tipped off to where the Chicago, Rock Island, and Pacific Railroad planned to run their tracks. He knew that in order to operate a successful cattle ranch, he was going to need access to grazing land, a railroad, and a good supply of water. But a prime location like this would cost $2.50 an acre in the Cherokee Outlet, the highest price there was of any homestead land. Walter believed that most settlers would be fighting over the bargain $0.50 and $1 acre plots, hoping to find something of value for next to nothing.

Walter didn't want anyone to know his plan, so he decided that as soon as the land rush began, he would head west along with the other homesteaders. He then would fall behind and, when the time was right, change direction and head northeast as fast as he could. He planned to stake a claim to his allotted 160 acres of land in an area located just outside of what would become a little town known as Enid, Oklahoma.

2. Sooners and Boomers

President Grover Cleveland officially designated September 16, 1893, as the day for the Cherokee Outlet to be opened to homesteading. People came from far and wide, hoping to find their little piece of heaven. They came by horseback, by train, by wagon, and by foot. At high noon, a cannon fired, signaling the start. More than 115,000 settlers rushed off to grab one of the forty-three thousand parcels of land. These people became known as "Boomers." Some tried to leave early to get to the best available land first. These people became known as "Sooners." Most of these were unsuccessful because the army had been called out to maintain order. There was a harsh punishment for anyone who tried to "jump the gun."

As soon as the cannon fired, Walter joined with the other Boomers in heading due west, but only at a moderate pace. He allowed the more determined settlers to pass him. When he thought the time was right, he changed direction and headed northeast just as he planned. As soon as he arrived in an area known as the North End, Walter went about marking his claim. This parcel of prime grazing land was west of Skeleton Creek and east of where there soon would be a train station. He surveyed his 160 acres and took these parameters to the land claims office. All he had to do now was to live there for at least six months and pay the designated price. Then all this land would be his. It sounded easy. Maybe too easy.

Walter McClain couldn't wait to relocate his family, but he needed to build a place for them to live. The only resources available to him were whatever was on his land. He had no money to buy lumber or hire workers. Everything he had was tied up in his homestead purchase. There were a few trees on his property, but they were quite spread out and difficult to harvest. He needed a place to live while he built his ranch house. Like most homesteaders at this time, Walter made what was called a dugout.

A dugout or sod house was nothing more than a large hole in the ground. The walls were built with stones and sod blocks to a height of seven or eight feet. Holes were left for doors and windows. Wooden poles supported the roof, which was made of a thick layer of grass. This sod would eventually grow together to make a somewhat solid roof. The floor was dirt with a few wooden planks. A small stove provided a little heat. It was cold, damp, dark, and muddy, but it was a place that the McClain family could call home, at least for a while.

Julie and the boys arrived soon afterward. This wasn't going to be the house on the hill with a white picket fence that they had dreamed about, but at least they were together as a family. It was a hard life, but they all did what they could. It took close to a year for Walter and the boys to build their ranch house while still riding fences and working the land. A cold winter slowed them down when food became scarce.

Before they could even move into their new home, Julie became sick. The cold and damp conditions were too harsh for her delicate body to withstand. She died of what they called consumption in the spring of 1894. Walter was never quite the same after that. For a short time, he believed that he had it all. He had finally built a home for his family, but if he couldn't share it with the woman he loved, it just didn't seem to matter. How could it? It would never be the same.

Walter, who had once been a very religious man, stopped going to Sunday prayer services. He said he couldn't abide by a God who would take away the only woman he had ever loved. Walter still sent his boys to Sunday school, but he felt that a part of him died that day and was buried along with his wife. Now he tended to keep to himself. He was always a good father to the boys, but he never had fun or laughed anymore. Junior and Butch had lost their mother, and now they could feel their father slipping away, too. They worried that they might have been the cause of some of their father's sadness and thought if they tried hard to be good boys, maybe it would go away. This only led to more frustration. There wasn't going to be an easy fix.

To help with raising the boys and to keep everything going, Doc decided to join Walter and the boys at their ranch outside Enid. He had also had enough of dusty cattle drives. Doc's presence was at first a reminder to Walter of his dear, departed bride. But after a period of adjustment, Doc fit right in. Walter and Doc had been like brothers during their cattle drive days, and it was easy for them to fall back into their old ways. Bad times are hard, but they don't last. Good friends last forever. The boys had only met Doc a few times due to his life on the trail, but he was family. He was their uncle, their mother's brother.

Walter told the boys that Doc could be loud and gruff at times. He might act like a tough cattle drive cowboy, but he was a nice guy once you got to know him. He just didn't want anybody to know it. He was a true old timer, slow moving but quick witted with a mind sharp as a knife. Doc liked to tell people there were more lines on his face than there were rivers and trails on a map of Oklahoma, and every one of them told a story. If you had the time, he would be glad to tell you about every one of them.

3. School Days

"Hey, Mark!" called Junior. "Let's see which one of us can hit that tall oak tree with a stone."

"You mean the big one on the other side of the creek?" replied Mark. "The one by Mr. Corbett's place? You know that he doesn't like to be bothered, and since everything bothers him, this might not be your best idea today."

"That tree is pretty far away," Junior said with a laugh. "The only thing you are going to bother are the fish in the creek when your stone splashes down into the water."

"You guys know that we don't have time for this," Butch said. "This is going to make us late. The last time we stopped on the way to school to play one of your silly games, it made us late. I'm not going to get my hand slapped with a ruler again because you guys made me late. No, not me, not again, no way."

Junior's given name was Walter McClain Jr. He was named after his father, Walter McClain Sr. Most people just called him Junior. Butch was Junior's little brother. Butch's name was Lamont McClain, but when he was a baby, a relative referred to him once as Butch, and the name stuck. Marquis Dupree was Junior's best friend. His mother had named him Marquis after the Revolutionary War hero Marquis de Lafayette. She thought that Marquis was the man's actual first name rather than a rank of royalty. Everybody called him Mark. Junior and Mark were both sixteen years old, but in their minds, they were grown men, ready to take on the world. Butch was thirteen. It was all he could do to keep up with the big boys.

Mark's father, Joseph Dupree, was a sharecropper from Louisiana, where his family had lived for generations. Times were hard, so he packed up his family and their meager belongings, and they joined the great migration west in search of a better life in Oklahoma. They farmed a little patch of land along Skeleton Creek across from Mr. Corbett's place. A man in town had told Joseph that he could get him a deed to this land at a special price. Joseph believed him and gave him his life savings. Needless to say, Joseph never saw the man or his money again.

Like many people from Louisiana, Mark's family was a combination of bayou Cajun and Delta Creole. The Cajun-Creole heritage was unique in that it contained various amounts of many assorted cultures and races. Mark's grandfather had once been a slave and his grandmother spoke fluent French. Mark's mother would often tease him that he might have a little bit of gator in him, too. Details like this didn't really matter to Mark and Junior. They had been buddies for as long as either could remember. They were partners, like Frank and Jesse James of the infamous bank robbing James gang. Mark and Junior were going to be the toughest desperadoes this side of the Rio Grande, just as long as this desperado thing didn't make them late for dinner.

On the prairie, you learned to adapt and make do with what you had. This was also true at school. The boys' schoolhouse was nothing more than four walls and a leaky roof. The class consisted of sixteen students of all ages. They sat on makeshift benches made from tree stumps. Lampblack was painted on pine slats to make a crude blackboard. The Oklahoma

Territory required that black, white, and Indian students all be taught in separate schools. The teacher tried to comply and even divided the class into their respective groups. Several students sat on one side of the room, a few more on the other side, and still more sat just outside the door, unless it rained. Junior and Butch sat with the white students, but Mark liked to make a game of it. He would change his seat every day, claiming he qualified to sit everywhere. He even tried to make his own group of one. It soon became obvious that almost as much time was spent separating the students as was instructing them. The teacher gave up and taught the class as one. They would all learn about segregation soon enough.

Junior searched the ground until he found the perfect stone. "OK, you sissy boys," he bragged, "watch and learn." Junior was big for his age and liked to show off his muscles. He gently tossed his stone into the air a few times and thought about how he was going to accomplish this magnificent feat of strength. When he was ready, Junior pulled back his arm as far as he could, took a few steps, and let his projectile fly high and far into the bright morning sky. As it approached the opposite side of the creek, the stone began to lose altitude. It landed with a splash and a thud, stuck in the mud at the very edge of the water. Although it certainly was a mighty throw, it landed well short of hitting the tall oak tree.

"Pay attention, fellows," Mark said with a laugh, "and I'll show you how it's done." Mark wasn't as big and strong as his friend but often found a way to out smart him just the same. He looked around and found just the right stone. It was flat, not round like Junior's had been. Mark twisted his body around and let his stone fly with an odd sidearm motion. About halfway across the creek, it began to slowly glide toward the water.

"Close, but not close enough," Junior said, "but as you can plainly see, I'm still the champion."

"Wait," Mark replied. "Wait for it." Just as the stone touched the water, something strange began to happen. The stone started to skip along the top of the water. One skip, two skips, three skips, and the stone had made it across the creek. It bounced off of a large boulder, flew over a patch of Indian blanket flowers, and landed with a bang at the base of the tall oak tree. "Ladies and gentlemen," Mark announced, "we have a new champion, and his name is Mark Dupree!"

"Who is that? Who goes there?" shouted Mr. Corbett. "I have a rifle, and I know how to use it. Identify yourself or prepare to face the consequences."

Mark and Junior took off running

toward school, laughing as they went. Butch tried desperately to keep up. The two older boys arrived at school first and waited for Butch.

"Butch," Junior said as his brother walked through the doorway, "if I've told you once, I've told you a million times. If you stop to play some game on the way to school, you are going to be late."

Butch just growled. Sometimes, it was hard to be the little guy.

4. Fishing Poles and Swimming Holes

"You know what, Mark? I think you cheated today. You didn't throw your stone across the creek," Junior said as the boys were walking home from school.

"Nobody said anything about throwing a stone," Mark said. "The rules only stated you had to hit the tall oak tree, and that's exactly what I did."

"How come you guys didn't let me try?" Butch complained. "I can throw a stone just as far as you guys, and—"

"Stop right there," Mark interrupted. "If you tried to throw a stone that far, you would have fallen into the creek, and then we would have had to explain to your dad how you took a soaker like that."

"Easy does it, Butch," Junior teased. "Today it's your turn to shovel dung in the barn, so if I were you, I would save all my energy for later."

"I'm going fishing," Mark said. "If you want to come along, I sure could use your help."

"How much help do you need from me to go fishing?" Junior asked. "I thought by now you'd have the hang of it. I can write down instructions for you if you'd like."

"No, wiseguy," Mark grumbled. "I'm going fishing to catch food for dinner. No fish, no food, so it's really important to catch as many as I can."

"OK, sure, no problem," Junior said, understanding that this wasn't going to be just another friendly fishing trip. This was business, and partners never let each other down. "I'll grab my pole and I'll meet you at the fishing hole. Hey, everybody, that rhymes!"

Junior met Mark at their favorite spot, where Skeleton Creek makes a big bend and the water was its deepest. This was also where they went swimming in the summertime because the water there was always cool and clear. It was a great spot to catch catfish, too, but you had to be patient and let them take your bait. If you didn't, you might yank the hook right out of their mouths. The boys had just started to fish when they noticed Mr. Corbett. He was standing alone on the opposite side of the creek.

"Easy does it. Don't run," Mark whispered. "You'll only spook him."

"Hey, boys," Corbett called from his side of the creek. "Did you happen to see anybody throwing stones at my place this morning?"

After a pause, Junior said, "N-n-no, Mr. Corbett, we didn't see anybody throwing stones. We walked straight to school today."

"Well, if you do," the old man said, "make sure to give them a message for me. Tell them that the next time they throw stones my way, they are going to be picking buckshot out of their butts for a week or maybe longer."

"No problem, M-M-Mr. Corbett," Junior stammered. "We'll be sure to say something if we see something or anybody or somebody."

As Corbett turned to leave, Junior whispered to Mark, "Do you think he knows it was us?"

"Of course he knows it was us," Mark said. "That's why he only gave us a warning.

If it had been anybody else who did it, they would be picking buckshot out of their butts for a week or maybe longer."

"When did you start stuttering?" Mark asked Junior, "I've never heard that from you before."

"I started stuttering right about the same time I started staring down at a crazy man with a shotgun pointed at me," Junior said.

The boys went about fishing, and today the catfish were biting. "Looks like the Dupree family will be having fish for dinner tonight," Junior said as he put another fish in his basket. "And tomorrow night and the next night and maybe the next one, too."

"Nothing ever goes to waste," replied Mark. "My mom will use them to make flapjacks, soup, biscuits, and everything else under the sun, and they always taste so good!"

The conversation then turned back to Mr. Corbett as Mark asked, "Do you know why Mr. Corbett is so mad all the time? He doesn't seem to mind it when we fish or swim in the creek, but other than that, he's always mad. He's mad when the sun comes up, he's mad when the sun goes down, and I'm pretty sure he's mad at all the time in between."

Junior thought about it and replied, "My uncle Doc said he served with Mr. Corbett in the Union army during the war, and he didn't like him much even back then. They both were on a detail searching for the assassin of President Abraham Lincoln. I read that a guy named Boston-something was the soldier who killed the assassin, but Doc says that just because you can read something in a book somewhere doesn't necessarily make it true. He said that Corbett had been a hat maker before the war and the chemicals he used must have ruined his mind."

"I bet that's what happened to the guy in the book we read in school, *Alice in Wonderland* by Lewis Carroll," Mark said. "They called him the Mad Hatter!"

"I must've been out that day," Junior said with a laugh, "or asleep."

Mr. Corbett's place wasn't much more than a dugout sod house, just like the one Walter McClain had built so many years ago. Corbett was born in London, England, in 1832. He came to America in 1839. He was employed as a hat maker before joining the army, and he was known to be more than a little strange. Everyone said that he was some kind of war hero, but lately it appeared as if he had sunk into some kind of insanity, believing that Confederate spies were out to get him as payback for what he had done in the war. Most folks thought he was crazy.

"Hey, Doc, what's for dinner?" Junior shouted as soon as he walked through the door.

"Beans and stew," Doc replied, "and warm biscuits from Mrs. Dupree." Doc would often take eggs, flour, and other things over to Mark's mother, and she would cook them up for him. He made sure to always bring enough for both families to share so he wouldn't have to cook that night and Mark's family would have dinner, too.

"We had beans and stew last night and the night before," Junior said.

"If you don't like my cooking," Doc replied, "you can go eat at Katie Walker's." Katie was a young widow who ran an eating establishment that served the best food in town. He husband had been killed by a stray bullet when a fight in Rosie's saloon spilled out into the street and bullets were flying everywhere.

"When we were out on the trail," Doc recalled, "the cowboys all loved my beans and stew, every last one of them. You can ask your father."

"But did they have to eat beans and stew every day?" asked Junior.

"Almost every day," Walter said. "Except for the days he made his stew and beans."

"I don't have to take this guff from you guys," Doc roared back. "You can all go eat at Katie Walker's place tonight. Go ahead and see if I care!"

Innocently, Butch asked, "Dad, do I have time to finish my homework before we leave for Mrs. Walker's?"

5. The Wichita Mountains Wildlife Refuge

Sometime late in the winter of 1898, word reached Walter McClain that the US Department of the Interior was planning to designate a wildlife refuge somewhere in the Wichita Mountain range of Oklahoma. The American buffalo was nearly extinct, and it was feared that the Texas longhorn might soon follow. They wanted to find a place where these animals and others like them could thrive and regenerate their herds. Rumor was that the government was willing to pay up to $25 a head for healthy longhorn breeding stock supplied in allotments of three males and forty-seven females. There would not be a cattle sale before April, so an opportunity like this meant unexpected cash to ranchers who were just trying to survive the winter. In order to conduct a livestock sale with the government, Walter had to meet each and every one of its exact requirements, the most important being proof that these animals were his to sell.

Back when this area was open grazing land, the buffalo roamed freely. Barbed wire soon crisscrossed the prairie, dividing the Great Plains into individual farms and ranches. If you purchased land, whatever wild animals that happened to be living on it were considered yours as well. Walter knew he had inherited several head of buffalo when he fenced in his land, but he had chosen to leave them alone. He didn't know how many there were by now, five years later, but his best guess was that there were probably a dozen or more of undetermined gender. However, they were scattered throughout his acreage. It might take a week or more to round them up and herd them into a corral.

Longhorns also had roamed this land. Kansas passed laws to prevent longhorns from entering the state because they carried a tick that was infected with Texas fever. Longhorns were immune to it, but it was fatal to the other short-horned cattle. Oklahoma ranchers often bred longhorns with their Angus or Herefords. This hybrid cow contained an even higher quality of beef product than any single type of cattle. Walter knew he had enough calves and young steers on hand to continue this hybrid breeding and still be able to sell off a large number of his adult longhorn stock for cash.

Walter told his boys about this upcoming special cattle sale one night at dinner. "Boys, it looks like I'm going to be away for a few nights to take care of some business," he said.

"Why is that, Daddy?" young Butch asked.

"I have to go to the territorial land headquarters in Guthrie," Walter said. "The federal government is going to designate an area of the Wichita Mountain range as a wildlife refuge. They want to gather up herds of buffalo, longhorns, some other animals that used to call this area home and maybe a few that still do and keep them in their own protected area. At the territorial land office, I can get a document that says our longhorns were either here when we bought the land or were born here while we owned it. They don't want cattle from Texas because they might carry the Texas fever tick. Longhorns are immune to it, but it could kill other animals."

"Why can't the land office in Guthrie talk to the government office conducting the sale and leave you out of it?" Junior asked.

"Because it's the government," Walter said, "and whenever they are involved, nothing ever gets done the easy way."

"So they don't want Texas longhorns from Texas," Butch said with an ironic laugh. "They only want Texas longhorns from Oklahoma."

"I think you're starting to get it," Junior said.

"The weather has been mild lately, so I don't think that's going to be a problem," Walter said to his boys. "But if we should get any snow, you two will have to load the wagon with hay, drive it out to the pasture, and unload it there or the livestock won't have anything to eat, and we won't have any cattle to sell."

Walter didn't show much emotion anymore, but he leaned over to Junior and tousled his hair. Then he motioned to Butch to come over and sit on his lap. "I'll be back in three days, tops!" he insisted as his voice got a little softer. "While I'm away, I don't want you two fighting and bothering Doc. He claims that his leg has been bothering him, and he's a little cranky. Doc says it's an old war injury, and I dare one of you to ask him about it. His story will last longer than my trip. And don't either of you two go bothering Mr. Corbett. Just leave that old boy alone."

6. Remember the *Maine*

At this same time, world events were taking place that would forever change the course of the McClain family's lives. Cuba had belonged to Spain ever since their explorers first inhabited the island in 1511. However, Cuba was now in the midst of a revolution. Rebels were fighting a war to free their land from foreign control. Most of the prevailing American opinions were on the side of these Cuban revolutionaries. Yellow journalists such as Joseph Pulitzer and William Randolph Hearst, filled their newspapers with inflammatory stories of Spanish atrocities against the Cuban people.

An artist named Frederic Remington was sent by Hearst to Havana to cover the Cuban insurrection. A story goes that he had contacted Hearst with the message, "There is nothing to report. There is no war here."

Hearst allegedly replied, "You furnish the pictures, and I'll furnish the war." It appeared that truth was also a casualty of war.

The next morning dawned sunny and warm. Although it was only mid-February, there was a feeling that spring must be just around the corner. Walter had already left on his trip to Guthrie. At breakfast, the only thing Junior and Butch talked about was going fishing after school. Doc expected to see the boys run in the door, throw down their books, grab their fishing poles, and run back out and down to the creek. It was going to be such a nice day that he figured he'd let them go. There would be time to do homework after dinner. They should get to enjoy the warm weather. Yesterday, Doc had cleaned and prepared a couple of chickens and given them to Mrs. Dupree to cook, so there was going to be chicken and biscuits for dinner. No beans and stew tonight.

That afternoon Junior ran through the doorway and right up to Doc. "Doc! Doc!" he cried. "They sunk the *Maine*. The *USS Maine* was anchored in Havana harbor, and they sunk it. They stuck a bomb to its hull while everybody was asleep. It exploded and killed around three hundred of the men on board. They sunk the *Maine*, Doc!"

By now, Butch had arrived and asked, "Doc, did you hear the news?"

"Yes, I did, son," he said. "But I need to slow everything down and think for a minute."

"The Spanish did it," Junior blurted out. "Everybody knows it. Mark and I talked about it, and we are going into town to volunteer. You know, sign up for the army or navy or something. We'll teach those Spaniards that they can't get away with killing Americans. We will make them sorry they were ever born."

"Slow down, slow it down," Doc pleaded, his hands raised in the air like he was stopping a wagon train. "You are ready to go to war, and you don't even know what to call it. When you join the army or navy, it's called enlistment, and son, you are too young to enlist. Maybe there is a way that your father can sign for you, but you'll have to wait until he gets home to talk it over with him."

"No, Doc," Junior protested. "They say that the Oklahoma birth records are so messed up that the army will take your word for it as long as you are willing to swear on a Bible you are old enough to join. It's that easy."

"Wait, you are going to swear on a Bible before God and tell a lie?" Doc said, surprised that the young man would even consider such an action. "You won't have to worry about going to Cuba. You will be go straight to hell."

"But, Doc, you went to war," Junior pleaded. "And you said God understood that you had to fight for your country. Now it's going to be my turn for adventure and glory."

Doc looked him straight in the eye and said, "Glory? Glory? You think there is something glorious about marching off to war?"

Doc asked the boys to sit down and spoke with them in a very serious voice. "Waiting a few days will give you and the Dupree boy a chance to cool down. I believe in answering the call when your country needs you, but let Mark talk to his father and you wait to talk with yours," Doc said, hoping he could cool the flames of war. "If they say it's OK, then I'll take you both into town myself, but waiting a few days won't hurt anything."

"Maybe there were times I might have made army life sound a little better than it really was," Doc explained, "but there is nothing glorious about sleeping in the mud and catching some kind of sickness that you can't even pronounce. I hate to have to say this, but sometimes my stories are just full of crap."

"That's OK, Doc," Butch said. "We always knew your stories were just full of crap."

"OK, Doc," Junior said. "I'll wait and talk to Dad first, but my mind is already made up. If my country is going to war, I have a responsibility to go and fight for my country."

7. The Blue Norther

The next morning dawned fair and warm. Butch looked over at Junior's bed and saw it was empty. He could tell that it hadn't been slept in, so he ran out to the kitchen to tell Doc. Butch looked around but couldn't find him anywhere. He began to call out, "Doc, Doc, are you here? Where are you?" Suddenly, he heard Doc's voice from somewhere outside.

"I'm out here, son," Doc said, "Come out here." Butch ran outside as fast as he could. He didn't know what was going on, but he knew he didn't like it.

"Doc, Doc," Butch exclaimed, "Junior isn't here, and his bed wasn't slept in, and I don't know where he is and..."

"Easy, pal, easy," Doc said, hoping to comfort the young man. "I'm sure he went into town with the Dupree boy to try to join the army. I figured he would. When that boy gets an idea inside his head, there's not much room for anything else. Right now we have a much bigger problem."

"A bigger problem than Junior went to join the army?" an excited Butch asked his uncle.

"Don't worry about Junior," Doc said. "His father is going to kill him long before the Spaniards can get a crack at him. Sooner or later, that boy has got to learn how to listen."

Doc leaned down to Butch and pointed to the northern sky. "Do you see that part of the sky over there that looks real, real dark?" Doc asked. "I've only seen it a few times in my life, but that's what is called a blue norther. The cold weather is moving so fast down through the Plains that you can actually see it coming towards you."

"What does that mean, Doc?" Butch asked. "And what do we have to do about it?"

"It's not just what we have to do," Doc insisted. "It's also about what you will have to do." They began walking toward the barn as Doc told Butch his plan. "First, we have to load the wagon with hay as fast as we can. I think we still have a few hours before the snow starts. Then you will have to take the load of hay out to the pasture and drop all the bales there so the cattle will have food to eat should the weather turn real bad. I'll hitch up the mules to the wagon. They're a little slower than horses, but they are stronger and smarter, too. I'm sure they will get you there and back home again in one piece."

There was so much going through Butch's mind that he couldn't think straight. He didn't know which question to ask first. "Wouldn't it be a better idea if you drove the wagon of hay out to the pasture and I stayed here?" Butch questioned.

"I can't," Doc answered. "Before I left the army, they told me I had rheumatism in my knees and hips. I think today they might call it arthur-itis or something like that. Your father knew that I wouldn't be able to take a long wagon ride. This is why he asked you and your brother to take the hay out to the cattle if the weather turned bad. Well, we're going to get the bad weather, but we don't have your brother. I know you can do it, Butch. I believe in you."

Butch paused a moment and asked, "Why did you say mules are smarter than horses, Doc?"

"You can get a horse to do almost anything you want it to do," Doc explained. "But if you try to do the same thing with a mule, that mule is going to have to think about it. You can run a horse right off a cliff, but try to do the same thing with a mule and that mule will probably stop and ask you to go first."

The wagon was loaded, and Butch was ready to go. Doc gave him a few last instructions. "Follow the creek until you get to the pasture. Dump your load and get out of there. I don't think you'll be able to make it back by nightfall. If you stop, make sure to untie the mules. Let them roam. They won't go far. Remember to save a little bit of hay for them. I don't think you'll have time to make a fire or pitch a tent, so find a place out of the wind and try to hunker down where you can. I put some blankets and a few biscuits from last night in the wagon for you. You've camped out on the trail before. It's easy."

Butch was about to climb into the wagon when he offered his right hand to Doc as if to shake hands. Doc took the hand, pulled him in close, and gave the young man a big bear hug. "There is nothing to it," Doc whispered. "You'll be fine."

Butch could already feel it starting to get colder as the wind swept the few leaves on the ground into little circles. Butch climbed into the seat of the wagon, gave the reins a shake, and said, "OK, let's go! See you tomorrow, Doc."

"See you tomorrow, son," Doc said as he watched the wagon roll away. Doc whispered to himself, "And God's speed, Butch. Be safe."

The sky was getting dark as Butch approached Skeleton Creek, and the rain began to fall. He knew that snow wouldn't be far behind. Butch thought he could save some valuable time if he crossed over the creek at the big bend and then crossed back over downstream near the pasture. The creek had many twists and turns, so much so that at times it was hard to tell which side you were on. He hoped that Doc's mules wouldn't mind getting a little wet. Butch liked his new plan, until he realized that it would take him right past Mr. Corbett's place.

8. Ice and Snow

Butch crossed over the creek right where he planned. It was shallow, and the mules didn't appear to mind the water too much. They actually seemed to be enjoying it as they splashed their way through the creek.

"Quiet down, you guys! Be quiet!" Butch ordered, hoping not to attract any attention. "If you give us away, Mr. Corbett will get even madder than he usually gets, and there will be hell to pay."

They rode across this strip of land as fast and as quietly as they could. Butch drove the wagon back across the creek as close to the pasture as he could find. The mules again were loud and playful, almost as if they were having fun splashing in the water.

"Go ahead and laugh it up," Butch scolded his mule team. "Have a good time, but just remember, I won't be the one who will be picking the buckshot out of your butts for a week." Butch could now see the steam from his breath as the wind blew an icy chill through his body. He pulled his hat down over his ears and buttoned his coat all the way up to the top.

Butch arrived at the pasture just as the rain was beginning to change to hail and freezing rain. Butch lowered the wagon's tailgate and started to push the bales of hay off the back as fast as he could. The freezing rain quickly coated everything with a glaze of ice. Butch slipped and fell a few times, finally pushing the last of the hay off the wagon with his legs while lying on his back. There were still two bales left, but they had already become frozen to the wagon bed and wouldn't budge. Butch knew that the livestock had enough to get by. He decided to ride back home with the tailgate down. If the last two bales fell off, that was OK. If they didn't, that was OK, too. Right now he didn't really care. The snow had started to fall so heavily that visibility was terrible. Butch decided to return the same way he had come. It was still the shortest and fastest way. He thought he should be all right because he couldn't imagine that Mr. Corbett would be out in a storm like this. Nobody was out in a storm like this, only him.

After getting back across the creek, Butch could see that the wagon's wheels and axles were starting to freeze up. Ice and snow now covered everything. Butch knew he would not be able to cross back over the creek again tonight or even travel much farther. He looked around, hoping to find a place where he could get out of the storm and perhaps clean off the wagon's frozen wheels.

The only thing Butch could make out through the falling snow was the distant shape of the little shack that stood next to Mr. Corbett's dugout. It was hardly a barn by any means, but it was where he kept his cow and a few chickens. It stood next to a small corral where Corbett kept his horse. Butch knew if he stayed where he was, it was likely that he wouldn't be found until the spring, no doubt frozen to the wagon. Going over to Mr. Corbett's place with a broken wagon and two noisy mules in a blizzard couldn't be any worse than that. It couldn't, could it?

Butch headed toward the shack. It was the only thing he could see, and he was even starting to lose sight of that as the snow intensified. His wheels locked up so badly that the mules had to pull the wagon like a sleigh sliding through the snow. When Butch arrived at the shack, he knocked hard on the door, but no one answered. He then went to the door of the dugout. "Hello, Mr. Corbett?" Butch called, trying to announce himself to anyone who might be inside. "It's only me, Butch McClain, Walter McClain's son. I got stranded out in this snowstorm, and I was hoping you might let me stay in your barn tonight." There was no answer. Butch saw that Mr. Corbett's horse was gone as well, so he assumed that nobody was home. Maybe they had also become stranded somewhere, or maybe they had gone to town.

A sense of relief came over the young man as he pushed the wagon into the shack. Butch knew he would have to face Mr. Corbett sooner or later, but later looked like it was the better of the two options. He untied the mules and let them nibble at the frozen hay that was still on the wagon. Butch wrapped himself up in his blankets and started to eat the biscuits Doc had packed for him. He found a soft spot to lay his head and fell right to sleep.

The next morning he awoke to the distinct sound of an approaching horse and rider. Butch swallowed hard and waited to learn his fate. The old hinges of the door squeaked loudly as it slowly opened. Suddenly, the shadow of a man appeared on the wall.

9. Visitors

Butch held his breath as he saw the unmistakable barrel of Mr. Corbett's Spencer repeating rifle slowly push its way into the room. "Who goes there?" Corbett demanded. "Identify yourself or prepare to face the consequences!"

"It's only me, Mr. Corbett," cried Butch. "Butch McClain. I was out in the snowstorm last night and got stranded and had to stay the night in your barn. You weren't here for me to ask permission, or I most certainly would have done so. I was all by myself, and I didn't know where else to turn."

Corbett studied the look on Butch's face long and hard, attempting to evaluate the boy's sincerity. Finally, he spoke. "I believe you. I've watched you kids playing and fishing, and you remind me of a time when my life was free and easy. I have no use for any of these other folks. They all want something from me, and I've already given everything I have. We'll keep this as our little secret. I don't want my place turning into some kind of stagecoach stop or railroad station. And don't go thinking that now you are welcome to come by anytime you please. You stay on your side of the creek and I'll stay on mine. The storm is almost over, so you had better get going."

Just as the tension appeared to ease, Butch heard the sound of additional men approaching on horseback. "If this is our good-for-nothing Sheriff Mason," Corbett said, "I might send him home with a little memento of his visit."

"Corbett? Corbett! We know you're in there!" insisted a voice from outside. It was the voice of Sherriff Mason. "You know why we're here, Corbett," Mason said. "You are a squatter on this land. You have no legal right to be here, and you will have to leave. I'm trying to do this with a little respect because I know you were in the war, but you have twenty-four hours to vacate the premises. There are some dark skinned undesirables around here who won't be getting this same courtesy." Another man dismounted and nailed an eviction notice to the wooden door of the shack.

With that, Corbett came out and spoke. "My, my! Where did you find this sad excuse for a posse, Sheriff? It looks like you rounded up this crew from Rosie's Saloon at closing time. I know who each one of you are and where you live. I see Big Pete, Little Pete, Fat Joe, and who is this scallywag hiding in the back? Could it be none other than Mr. David George? It must be. Who else would hide out in the rear and let other people do his fighting for him? You are trying to hide from me because I know who you really are. You've been nothing but trouble for me every day of my life. I should have taken care of you back when I first had the chance. You can bet your pretty new boots that I won't make that same mistake again."

Corbett spit on the ground and wiped his brow. He loaded a live round into the chamber of his rifle and fired a shot in the air. Corbett turned and ripped the eviction notice off the door and threw it on the ground.

"You'll be sorry you did that," the sheriff said. "We'll be back, and you'll be wishing that you had left when you had the chance."

"I don't see nobody here man enough to make me leave," Corbett declared. "But you are all welcome to try. I got seven shots in my rifle and six more in my revolver. That means, that means I got…"

From inside the barn, he heard Butch whisper, "That makes thirteen shots, Mr. Corbett."

"That means I got thirteen shots, thirteen reasons why some of you boys won't be riding back home." He turned and gave Butch a wink. The sheriff and his men rode away with a promise that they would be back, and this time they would mean business.

"The sky is starting to clear," Corbett said, "so you'd better get yourself on home, boy. Get home just as fast as you can. There is going to be some trouble around here, and you don't need to be any part of it. You are a young man. Life is going to give you your own fair share of trouble. You don't need more."

"Thanks, Mr. Corbett," Butch said. "I left two bales of hay in your barn for letting me stay here. They are still a little frozen, but they will be OK as soon as they thaw out. I promise I will get home just as fast as my mules can take me."

As Butch rode away, Corbett smiled a little smile and said to himself, "Fast mules? Now that's something I would really like to see."

10. The Return Home

Walter and Junior were already home by the time Butch arrived. He was glad to see them and wanted to hear all about their adventures, but Butch couldn't wait to find out what had happened to his brother and Mark in town.

"Junior," Butch said, "are you in the army now? Are you going to Cuba?"

"No," said Junior, "or at least not yet. The army soldiers were willing to sign me up right away, but they didn't want to sign Mark. They kept telling him they weren't looking for any Buffalo Soldiers, whatever that means, and he should try coming back tomorrow. Then they said it again to him this morning. Finally, we both decided to come home."

"But if they wanted you," Butch asked, "why didn't you just go enlist by yourself?"

Junior paused for a moment and said, "Because Doc once told me that a soldier never leaves another soldier behind on the battlefield. Some of the words they said to Mark were, well, not very Christian-like. It was almost as if some of them were at war with Mark rather than with Spain. I was not going to leave him behind. We decided either we both stay or we both leave. Whatever we were going to do, we would do it together."

Walter's face slowly turned a crimson red. He looked Junior straight in the eye and said, "Your uncle told you not to go into town to enlist, that you should wait until I got back, but you didn't listen to him. You can say whatever you want about your responsibility to a comrade on the battlefield. As far as I am concerned, you had a responsibility right here, and you deserted your post. You were needed to help get feed out to the cattle, but you went missing."

Junior had nothing to say. He just stared at the floor and mumbled a few times as his father continued.

"I understand that you felt a duty to your country, but what about your duty to your family? If anything had happened to your little brother, it would have been your fault. I hope you can live with that." Tears ran down Junior's cheeks as his father gave him his punishment. "Since your brother did your share of work getting the hay out to the livestock, you will do his share of work cleaning dung out of the barn for the next two months. Any questions?"

"No, sir," Junior said, hoping this would soon would be over.

Butch looked at Junior, smiled, and whispered, "Why, hello there, Mr. Dung Man!"

Junior just mumbled, "Oh, you shut up."

"I had a little better luck in Guthrie," Walter said. "The Department of the Interior will buy fifty head of longhorns from us as long as we can provide them with the three males and forty-seven females they requested. They will take all the buffalo we can find. The government man said buffalo have been practically wiped out. They're almost extinct."

"How much are they going to pay, Walter?" Doc asked.

"They will pay twenty-five dollars a head for adult longhorns," Walter said, "and twenty dollars a head for all buffalo we can find of any age or gender."

"Just as long as they are Texas longhorns from Oklahoma and not Texas longhorns from Texas!" Butch added, retelling his joke.

Then it was time for Butch to tell his story. "Doc said we were going to get a blue norther, so we loaded up the wagon with hay, and I took it out to the pasture. The weather was turning bad real fast, so I cut across the creek right where it is shallow and then back over again by the pasture. I unloaded the hay and tried to head home, but the wheels froze to the axles in the snow. I had to spend the night at Mr. Corbett's place."

"Mr. Corbett's place!" all three family members uttered at once.

"He wasn't home, so I slept in his little barn. I left him two bales of hay as payment. He got home before I left, but he wasn't too mad. But then the sheriff showed up with a posse and a guy named Mr. George. They said they were evicting anyone who didn't have a deed to their land. Can they do that, dad?"

"I'm not sure," Walter said. "But nobody wants to argue with the barrel of a gun. Corbett can take care of himself, but there are others who won't be so lucky if the sheriff follows through with this. It could get worse before it's over."

As they walked, away Butch asked Doc, "Why did they tell Mark that they weren't looking for any Buffalo Soldiers?"

Doc stopped, looked at Butch and said, "Buffalo Soldier is a name Indians gave to army soldiers with dark skin. Although Mark's family is a mix of races, he's not white. His skin is dark and that's all some ignorant people can see." He could see that his nephew was becoming a young man, trying to understand the world around him.

"All he wanted to do was join the army," Butch said, "to fight and maybe die for his country. Why isn't that enough, Doc?"

"Because we live in a crazy world." Doc replied. "Maybe things will change some day but if I were you, I wouldn't hold my breathe waiting for it to happen."

11. Troubled Times

After dinner, Junior and Butch got busy with their homework while Walter and Doc cleaned up in the kitchen. "You know, Walter," Doc said, "I hate to bring up this subject, but it's been on my mind for a while now."

"You are going to bring it up anyway, so go ahead." Walter said.

"You know I can't keep quiet when there is something that needs to be said," Doc stated, trying to look real serious as he continued. "You know, Julie's been gone four years now. She was my little sister, and

I miss her something terrible. But four years is a long time to grieve. You are still a young man. Don't you think it's time for you to pay a call on some nice lady? Somebody like Katie Walker? She is sweet and very pretty. We all know she is a great cook, too."

"You make a good point, Doc," Walter said, patting his friend on his back. "And if I married Katie Walker, we wouldn't have to eat your beans and stew anymore."

"Dagnabbit," Doc shouted. "I'm trying to be serious here. Pay attention!"

"I am being serious, Doc," Walter said. "I believe that a man is fortunate if he can find true love once in his life. I also believe that the likelihood of the same man finding true love twice in his life, to love someone two times with all your heart and soul, is like wishing on a rainbow. No matter how many times you wish, there's never going to be a pot of gold at the rainbow's end. Dreams and wishes don't come true,"

Walter said. He could still feel the emptiness inside where his love for Julie had once resided, and he wondered if his broken heart would ever mend.

"If you are fool enough to believe there will be a pot of real gold waiting for you at the rainbow's end, then of course you're right," Doc said, "but a pot of gold can be many things. It can be your friends, your family, your happiness, and you might not have to wish for it. It may have been right in front of you all along."

Walter paused a moment and said, "I'll think about it. That's all I can say."

Butch suddenly ran into the room, bursting with something to say. "I saw lights out on the road, flickering lights, like when something's burning," he said. "What do you think it could be?"

Doc looked over at Walter and said, "They've been trying to run people off their land, anyone who they think won't fight back. They still can't accept the fact that the war is over and done."

"If somebody doesn't belong on their land, then let a court say so," Walter said. "But I don't want some posse of drunks taking the law into their own hands. Hitch up the horses, Doc, and not those slowpoke mules of yours. I want to get there tonight. I'll grab the shotguns and meet you outside. I hope they won't be necessary. OK, let's go."

"Junior, Butch," Walter said as if directing men on a cattle drive. "Listen to me and do exactly what I say. There might be some trouble tonight over at the Dupree place. Doc and I are going over there to see if we can help keep things from getting out of hand. I want you two to stay right here. I repeat, stay here. Do you understand?"

"Yes, sir, Dad," Butch answered. "I understand."

Walter then pointed at Junior and said, "Now let me hear it from you."

"Yes, I understand," Junior said. "I'll stay here, no matter what happens."

Doc's voice could be heard from outside of the house. "If we're going, let's go. My mules could have been there and back already. Who's the slowpoke now?" Walter ran outside, climbed onto the wagon, and they were gone.

"What're we going to do, Junior?" Butch asked. "Dad said to stay here."

Junior thought about it for a minute and said, "What are we going to do? I'll tell you what I'm going to do. I'm going to give Dad and Doc a five-minute head start. Then I'm going to run along the creek until I get to the Dupree place. If something's going to happen to Mark tonight, I have to be there with him. We are partners, through thick and thin. If he needs me, I've got to go."

Butch was confused and didn't know which way to turn. He tried to reason with his big brother. "If you disobey Dad again, he's going to whoop your butt. You will be shoveling dung for the rest of your life, or maybe longer."

"I'll have to cross that bridge when I get to it," Junior said. "I am leaving. Decide now if you are staying here, or coming with me?"

"I'm coming! I'm coming," Butch said with some uncertainty. "I only hope that Dad will be so tired from giving you such a big whooping that maybe mine won't be so bad."

12. The Showdown

Walter and Doc rode as fast as they could. They hoped to get to the Dupree place before there was any trouble. Walter felt like the wagon wasn't moving as fast as it should, so her asked Doc, "What's the matter with these horses? Why are they moving so slowly?" Doc didn't answer right away, so Walter began to look around. Finally, he spotted the problem. "You didn't hitch up the horses like I had asked you to," Walter said. "You hitched up those lousy mules again!"

Doc tried to calm him down. "I heard what you said, but horses are only fast on a road. If we have to travel over land, my mules will get us there faster."

Walter just shook his head and said, "Your mules! I hate your mules! Sometimes you can actually do the impossible. You can make me wish I was back on a cattle drive again."

They arrived only minutes ahead of the posse. Mark's father, Joseph, stood in his doorway holding an ax. Doc and Walter climbed down from the wagon and ran right over to him.

"Thank you for coming here," Joseph said, "but I don't need anybody to fight my fights for me."

"We're not here to fight," Walter said. "We're only here to try to keep the peace, and make sure there isn't any trouble."

When the posse arrived, a man who appeared to be their leader addressed

Walter and Doc. "You two men have no business here. These people don't belong on this land, and we are here to see that they leave in a nice, orderly fashion, if you know what we mean."

"If these people have no right to this land," Walter shouted, "tell the sheriff and have him get a court order that says so and give these people due process. We won't stand in your way as long as you do it by the law."

"I suspect Sheriff Mason is already here," said Doc. "He's hiding somewhere in the rear because he's a gutless, yellow-bellied coward."

With that, the sheriff came forward and said, "Doc, you'd better learn to shut your mouth, or I'll shut it up for you myself!"

Junior and Butch appeared from out of the darkness and took a position next to their father.

"I knew it. I knew you wouldn't listen to me, Junior," Walter said. "And now you've dragged your little brother into this, too."

At that moment, Mark came out of the house and stood between his father and Junior.

Doc looked at the posse, spit on the ground, and said, "Well, if you boys came here tonight looking for a fight, I believe you came to the right place. We'd be happy to oblige."

The leader moved closer, got off his horse and said, "We are going to do exactly what we came here to do. We are going to teach these people a lesson. They don't have a deed to this land. Besides, dark skin folks aren't welcome around here. Stand in our way, and you will become a part of that lesson."

One of the horsemen dismounted and started to move toward the house with a burning torch in his hand. Walter pointed his shotgun at him and said, "Stop right there. Don't make another move, or I'll teach you a lesson myself."

The leader raised his hand for the man to stop and said, "All I see here is two boys, two men, and a family who should still be slaves if I had my way," the leader said. "You have two guns. I have eight men, each one armed and ready. You'd better step aside. Now! I am giving you your final warning."

Suddenly, a loud voice rang out from the darkness. "You boys must have forgotten about me!" the voice said. "And let he who is without sin cast the first stone!"

"Who's that?" someone said. "Where is that voice coming from?"

"I have a Colt revolver and a Spenser rifle," the voice declared. "My partner says that makes thirteen shots. Prepare to suffer the consequences of your actions."

"It's Mr. Corbett!" Butch exclaimed. "He's come to help us!"

"I know who you are, you scum," Corbett shouted to the leader. "Which one of your names are you going by today? Are you going by Mr. John St. Helen? Or are you going by Mr. David E. George?"

The leader paused for a moment and replied, "And what name are you going by tonight, Mr. Thomas 'Boston' Corbett?"

"Boston Corbett, Lincoln's avenger?" a shocked Sheriff Mason said.

"He's the guy!" Junior exclaimed. "He's the guy who shot the guy who shot the other guy, the president, President Lincoln."

Corbett then called out to the leader, "I have you dead in my sights. The last thing you will see and hear on this earth will be my shot hitting you right between your eyes. Your blood will be all over your pretty new boots. I still have the sixteen missing pages from your diary. I'll be sure to put them on your grave."

The posse began to stir as their leader tried to regain control. "Don't listen to him. He's nothing but a crazy old man who doesn't know what he's talking about."

Corbett paused, loaded his rifle, and said, "What name do you want on your tombstone? Do you want John St. Helen or David E. George? Or do you want me to put your God-given name on it? I'll see you in hell tonight, Mr. John Wilkes Booth."

Everybody gasped all at once. A startled Sheriff Mason tried to regain his composure and said, "I'm not sure exactly what's gone on here tonight. I'm going to need a little time to think this over. We're going to leave, but we'll be back in the morning with a court order for these people to vacate the premises, and when I do I don't expect to get any trouble from you, Walter McClain."

"If everything is legal, you'll get no trouble," Walter said. "But remember to bring a US marshal with you when you come. This is still federal land, so you will need a federal lawman to perform a legal eviction."

"It's going to take me four days to get a US marshal here!" the sheriff protested.

"Then if I were you," Doc said with a chuckle, "I'd get busy doing my job for a change."

"I'm no preacher man," Walter said, "and as far as I am concerned, you are all welcome to like or hate whoever you choose. Everyone will have to work that out on your own. But if you ever want to see this territory granted statehood, we've got to show the other states and the world that the people of Oklahoma are civilized and law abiding. There has to be an end to the Wild West."

As the posse left, Joseph Dupree shook hands with Walter and Doc and said, "I want to thank you gentlemen for saving my family tonight."

"You should thank Corbett if you can find him," Walter said. "He made the difference. Whatever he said, it sure scared the bejesus out of that guy. John Wilkes Booth! Really? What on earth will they think of next?"

Joseph looked around for a moment and said, "We are going to be moving along. I don't have a deed to this land, and you can bet they will be back sometime soon, court order or not."

"How will you travel?" Doc asked. "Where are you going to go?"

"We have a horse," Joseph said. "We we will pack up whatever we can and head west."

"I have a proposition for you," Walter said. "Please take this old wagon. It's a Conestoga, so you know it's sturdy. It still has the truss for a canvas roof if you can rig up some poles. I do have one condition, though. You have to take these mules with it, too."

"My mules!" Doc exclaimed. "Not my mules!"

"Thank you, but we don't take charity," Joseph said. "We'll find a way to make it on our own. We always have, and we always will."

"Don't look at this as charity. It's a loan," Walter said. "Whenever you get where you are going, somewhere with your feet on the ground, you can return it to me. But only the wagon, not the mules. They're my gift to you. Keep them, please keep them."

Mark walked up to Junior and said, "Good luck, partner. I never got to teach you how to skip a stone. Maybe your next partner will be able to show you how it's done."

"I'm never going to have another partner like you," Junior said.

"Maybe we'll meet up again," Mark said. "And we'll ride the prairie just like we always planned."

"My dad says I shouldn't go wishing for things that can never come true," Junior said. "He says you should't waste your time wishing on a rainbow because no matter how hard you wish, there is never going to be a pot of gold. You might just as well save your time."

"He may be right," Mark said. "But if there was ever going to be two guys who can make wishing on a rainbow come true, it will be us. Sometimes the impossible can come true. It just takes a little faith. You've got to believe."

The two best friends gave each other a handshake, a hug, and a wave, and Junior disappeared into the darkness.

13. Wishing On a Rainbow

Junior never did see Mark again, although he always hoped that he would. Walter never saw his wagon, and Doc never saw his mules. Sometimes things happen that are out of your control, and the only option you have is to just let it be. Every now and then, just before he went to sleep, Junior would say a little prayer for his friend Mark and his family, wishing them health and happiness. He often wondered if Mark might be somewhere, looking up at the same stars and wishing the same thing for him. After all, they were partners, through thick and thin.

School was over, and Junior had some big decisions to make about his future. One night at dinner, Walter asked his son, "Have you given any thought to what you want to do? There are quite a few options available to you."

"I have been giving it some thought," Junior replied. "It's been on my mind for a while now, and I'm pretty sure I know what I am going to do."

Before he had a chance to say much more, Doc jumped into the discussion. "There are quite a few good schools now in Oklahoma. The Territorial University is in Norman. The school of agriculture is in Stillwater. There is even a Normal School in Edmond for teachers."

"Thanks, everyone," Junior said. "Dad, I know I'm still too young to enlist in the army, but we can talk about it again in another year or so."

"That's all I ever wanted. That's all I ever asked from you," Walter said.

"But until then," Junior continued, "the *Enid Eagle* newspaper is going from a weekly to a daily publication, so they have quite a few jobs that need to be filled. They said I can start as an apprentice, but if I work hard, I will have an opportunity to move up. This is the future, and I want to be a part of it."

Everybody went quiet for a minute or two. Doc broke the silence as he said, "Does anybody want some more stew? How about some more beans?"

Walter put his knife and fork down and looked at his son. "The newspaper industry is a fine business, and it's growing just as fast as the state of Oklahoma. You will have to start at the bottom, carrying reams of paper and inking printing presses, but hard work never hurt anyone. It helps you appreciate a good job all the more."

"Thank you, Dad," Junior said. "I didn't know what you were going to say. I was worried that if I didn't go into ranching like you or the army like Doc, I might be letting you down."

Walter looked at his son and said, "You are a fine young man, and I am proud to call you my son. I wish you'd listen to me a little more, but you are my boy, and I will always love you. To think that you could ever let me down is like, well, like wishing on a rainbow. You can do all the wishing you want, but it won't change a thing."

Junior got up from the table, wiped away a tear, and gave his father a hug like never before. "I love you, too, Dad," he said, speaking from his heart. Walter thought about what a fine young man his boy had become and said, "And there is one more thing. Your mother is looking down on you tonight, and she is just as proud of you as I am."

After a few moments, Butch said, "Dad, I think I want to talk to you about something, too."

"I don't think my heart can take two of these in one night," Walter said, "but go ahead, son. Let me have it. Tell me what's on your mind?"

"I heard you and Doc talking a while ago about the possibility of you keeping company with Mrs. Walker," Butch said, "and I was wondering if you would mind if I ask her daughter Beth to go fishing with me. She is pretty and smart and nice, and she likes fishing, too."

"Butch," Walter said, scratching his head, "why on earth would I mind if you asked the little Walker girl to go fishing with you?"

"Because," Butch said, "if you were to marry her mother, that would make her my sister, and that is just too weird for me."

"You know," Doc said, "the boy may have a point there. This might take a little figuring out."

"I am not keeping company with Katie Walker," Walter said with a laugh, a laugh that had been missing from his life for a long, long time. "Katie Walker and I have no plans to get married or anything. I can promise you that Beth Walker will never be your sister. Don't give it another thought. Please feel free to go fishing with Beth Walker, or take her picking wildflowers, or maybe even buy her a sarsaparilla. It's all OK with me."

While the boys were cleaning up after dinner, Junior casually asked Butch a question. "Does Beth Walker know how to cook as good as her mother? You know, can she make something besides beans and stew?"

The boys heard Doc holler from the other room, "I heard that, you little whippersnappers!" It was good to be home.

14. Epilogue

Later that same year, a person in Enid, Oklahoma, filed an application to receive army pension benefits in the name of Thomas Corbett. After a thorough investigation by the government, it was decided that this person could not prove his identity, and the application was rejected. The few people who actually knew Thomas "Boston" Corbett claim that he had moved to Hinckley, Minnesota, where it is believed that he perished on September 1, 1894, when a great fire destroyed much of the surrounding forest. Although a Thomas Corbett was listed among the dead and missing, and practically everyone who has ever looked into this situation believes that this person was indeed the same Boston Corbett, there is still no absolute proof of his identity. There will always be people who believe he is buried in an unmarked grave in a potter's field somewhere in Enid, Oklahoma.

Every history book will tell you that John Wilkes Booth died in Port Royal, Virginia, on April 26, 1865. While he was hiding out in a tobacco barn, Union soldiers surrounded the building. When he refused to surrender, the soldiers set the barn ablaze. Booth died of a bullet wound to his neck, fired from the gun of one Sergeant Boston Corbett. His body was taken to Washington, DC, where it was positively identified as that of John Wilkes Booth by his mother, family members, friends, and even his dentist. A personal diary was found on him, but sixteen critical pages that could have shed some light on the conspiracy, assassination, and attempted escape were mysteriously missing from it. His body was laid to rest in the Booth family plot at the Green Mount Cemetery in Baltimore, Maryland.

A man by the name of John St. Helen had moved to Granbury, Texas, from parts unknown. After falling ill and believing that he would soon die, he made a deathbed confession that he was not who he had claimed to be but was actually the fugitive John Wilkes Booth. However, after making an unexpected recovery, he decided to flee. His travels eventually took him to Enid, Oklahoma, but now under the alias of David E. George. Local newspapers reported that a man named David E. George committed suicide by strychnine poisoning in room four of the Grand Hotel of Enid in January 1903. Strychnine is known to cause an agonizing death, and people who heard the man's screams and moans rushed to his bedside in an attempt to help the dying man. They were all quite shocked to hear his deathbed confession that he was indeed Abraham Lincoln's assassin, John Wilkes Booth.

Everybody will tell you that Thomas "Boston" Corbett died in a fire in the woods outside of Hinckley, Minnesota, and this is where his remains lie scattered today. Everybody will also tell you that John Wilkes Booth was shot and killed in Virginia as he attempted to flee from Union soldiers, who were in pursuit of him after he shot and killed President Abraham Lincoln, and he is buried today in a Baltimore, Maryland, cemetery.

What about Enid, Oklahoma? Everybody will tell you that the city has no connection at all to either of these two men. These items are nothing more than interesting coincidences. But as Doc used to say, just because you read something in a book somewhere doesn't necessarily make it true, now does it?

ABOUT THE AUTHOR

Thomas Yorke resides in Toms River, New Jersey with his wife, Nancy. Together they have two children, two granddaughters, with another grandchild on the way. He recently retired from a major research and engineering company after thirty two years. Thomas has authored many articles and papers for leading industry publications. He recently published a collection of short stories titled *Milepost Zero.* You can email Thomas Yorke at tomyorke1@verizon.net

Also Available from Thomas Yorke

Milepost Zero

Sometimes milepost zero is the end of a long journey. Other times it's the first step of a new adventure. Once in a while, it's a place to stop and look around, see where you've been and where you are going. *Milepost Zero* is a collection of suspenseful, funny and heartwarming coming-of-age stories about the decisions you make and how they shape the life you lead. It's about the legends and lore of living in a place some call paradise, Key West. Be careful. One person's heaven is another one's hell.

Available now from Amazon in paperback or Kindle

http://www.amazon.com/Milepost-Zero-Thomas-Yorke/dp/1511582162/ref=sr_1_1?s=books&ie=UTF8&qid=1430921387&sr=1-1&keywords=Thomas+Yorke

Help find a cure for MS. Please give to
The National Multiple Sclerosis Society